CW01468658

Wife Swapping Party - A Wife Watching Multiple Partner Hotwife Romance Novel

Karly Violet

Published by Karly Violet, 2021.

This is a work of fiction. Similarities to real people, places, or events are entirely coincidental.

WIFE SWAPPING PARTY - A WIFE WATCHING MULTIPLE PARTNER HOTWIFE ROMANCE NOVEL

First edition. September 13, 2021.

Written by Karly Violet.

Wife Swapping Party

A Wife Watching Multiple Partner Hotwife Romance Novel

Chapter One: A Warm Reception

"Over there," Marcy says as she points toward the corner of the living room. "We'll worry about unboxing the books later." I nod my head and carry the box to the corner and put it down.

"The bookshelf for these has to be somewhere around here," I tell her. "The movers weren't exactly worried about putting things where they belonged, were they?"

"They were definitely in a hurry," my wife replies. "Here, help me with these." She picks up two curtain rods and nods toward the windows. "I think they have the same kind of brackets, so it should be easy to hang them."

"Is the bed in the bathroom?" I joke as I carry one of the curtain rods to the window. "I mean, it wouldn't surprise me."

Marcy giggles. "We probably shouldn't have paid them the rest of that money until they got things where they needed to be."

"They had a certain odor to them, though, right? Did you really want to have them stick around much longer?"

"Uh, no." We both laugh as we work on the curtains in the living room. Even though our belongings are spread across the house without rhyme or reason, my wife and I are very happy to be moved in finally. It took some work to get things going once I got the transfer approval from Boston's corporate office to Miami. Instead of cold, blustery winters, we will now enjoy near-Caribbean weather the majority of the year.

Marcy scrunches her nose as she looks at the curtains we have just put up. "One of them looks a little crooked, Jake. I would swear to it."

Looking at it myself, I have to agree with her. "I'll work on straightening it later. For now, we need to get as many of our things put away somewhere before I have to leave for work in a couple of days."

My wife walks over to me and gives me a tight hug. "I just want to say how proud I am of you, baby. You went into Mr. Sandberg's office and told him that you wanted a better position, and now here you are. Who would have thought a year ago that we would be in a gated community in Miami, Florida?" Marcy pulls my head down toward her and kisses me lightly on the lips before turning to pull something else out of a box. It's now that I admire her petite form. At five-three and less than a hundred pounds, my blonde-haired, green-eyed woman is a hot spinner at just thirty years old. I'm truly a lucky man to know her and to have her as my own, so taking a chance with Mr. Sandberg to get him to send us to Miami and make her the happiest woman in the world was well worth it.

There's a knock at the door and we look at each other as if questioning who could be there. I walk toward the door and open it to find two other people, a man and a woman appearing to be not much older than us, standing there with a plate of cookies in their hands.

"Well, hello," the woman says before I can properly greet the two of them.

"Hello," I answer as I smile and nod my head.

"We're the Campbell's from next door. I'm Sadie and this is Luke." She offers me her hand as she steadies a plate of cookies in her other hand. I shake it and nod my head before I turn and shake her husband's hand.

"I'm Jake," I reply. Turning and motioning to my wife, I add, "This is my wife, Marcy." I stand aside as our neighbors walk into our messy living room.

"Hi. It's great to meet you," Marcy tells them as she walks up to the couple. She gives Sadie a quick side-hug and then shakes the other man's hand. It's at this moment that I realize that Sadie isn't wearing a bra, her B-cup size breasts pointing hard through the thin tee shirt she is wearing. There's no doubt that she has large nipples and that she could be a bit cold.

"We were debating whether to come over," Luke says as he closes our door. "We made a fresh batch of cookies and thought you might like something to snack on while you're working over here. It's my grandmother's recipe." He smiles as he nods his blond head toward us. The bulge in his tight shorts quickly catches the eyes of my wife and I

almost chuckle at the sight of her trying to avoid looking at it. There is
very little left to the imagination with our neighbors' bodies.

"We're glad you did," Marcy replies. "Cookies are just what we
needed." She takes the two plates and puts them down on one of the large
boxes in the living room. "We would offer you a place to sit down, but as
you can see, the movers left us a little out of sorts."

"Ah, the drop and go," Luke replies. "I think our movers did the same
thing when they brought our things here a few years ago."

"Definitely," Sadie confirms. "Maybe the same ones?"

"Maybe," I say with a smile and nod. "They definitely won't be
getting any more work from us, though. Not that we plan to move again
for a while."

"I hope not," Sadie replies as she smiles at me. Her blue eyes are
intense as she stares at me. My cock stiffens a little as I think about how
attractive she is, especially with the tight shirt she is wearing. Surely she
knows that she is displaying her nipples for all to see.

"I think you'll find this is a great neighborhood," Luke tells us. "We
are very tight-knit and look out for each other around here. That makes
things even safer for us all along with the fact that we are a gated
community. No one gets in here without someone knowing." He smiles
before asking, "Do you both enjoy nightlife?"

"Nightlife? You mean, bars and clubs?"

"Not really," Sadie chimes in. "He means getting to know your
neighbors through street parties and such. We even have a few other
events where we get together and just hang out for entire weekends."

"Wow," my wife replies with a smile. Marcy loves to get to know
other people. Perhaps this is her opportunity to make some new friends.
"Do you both go to these parties?"

"All of them," Sadie answers. "We help to plan a lot of them too. It's
a great time, I can promise you that."

"We look forward to it, then," I say as I smile at the two of them. Like Marcy, I am having difficulty avoiding gazing at both of their obvious assets.

"Great. Then we should let the two of you get back to work. If you need any help, we are in the house right next door." Luke points to the window where just a short distance away stands a very nice brick home. "We are there a lot, even throughout the day."

"We work from home," Sadie adds. "Our schedules are pretty flexible if you should need anything." She looks at me and winks before turning with her husband to go to the door.

"It's been great meeting you," Marcy tells them. They walk through the front door and close it behind them, leaving us to wonder about our new neighbors.

"That was odd," I say with a chuckle. "Did you see her nipples?"

"And his dick," my wife giggles. "They're both showing off. I would swear to it."

"Showing off?" I shake my head. "They probably just enjoy wearing clothes like that. I don't think they would have come over here to meet us while purposely showing off their bodies to us."

"Sadie winked at you," Marcy points out.

"Oh, you saw that?" I reply as my face turns hot.

"Yeah, I saw it." She laughs. "You have a way with the ladies, don't you?"

"I guess so." Marcy's wicked smile causes me to shake my head. "Oh, come on. She didn't mean anything by it."

"Sure she didn't. Anyway, Luke's packing heat, isn't he?" My wife appears to enjoy pointing out this fact to me.

"It's probably a pair of rolled up socks he shoved into his pants to get that effect," I joke. "I mean, he can't be *that* large."

"It seems that he's that large, Jake. Maybe you need to order some of those enhancement pills for yourself so that you can sport a huge bulge like Luke's."

"Or maybe I could just go get a large, thick pair of socks to roll up and cram into my pants." We both laugh as we talk about our new neighbors. There's something different about Luke and Sadie Campbell besides the way they happen to dress. Their attitudes seemed exceptionally curious and inviting. It was almost as if they were trying to size us up for something they plan to do.

"Dare I say they are a creepy couple?"

"*Creepy?* Nah, just eccentric. And the parties here? Are there really as many as they claim?"

My wife shrugs her shoulders. "The real estate agent didn't mention that there were parties around here. Surely that would have been a selling feature if she knew about them, right?"

"I would think so," I agree. "But the Campbell's said there are parties. Here's your chance to get to know some people and make new friends, Marcy."

"Not quite like the ones I had," she laments. "I'm already missing Tabitha and Sandra. They were like sisters to me."

"I know." I walk over to her and put an arm around her. "But you'll find more friends here. Who knows, maybe Sadie will have you leaving your bra at home soon?"

Marcy laughs. "Not likely, Jake." We kiss before turning to get back to work putting things away. There is a lot to learn about our new community here, but first we have to get our own home in order. Once we do, then it will be a good time to relax a little.

Chapter Two: Neighborhood Tour

"Sweetie." I turn to see Marcy standing in the doorway of our bedroom as I put on my shirt after having a morning shower. "We have company." Her eyes tell me that our visitor is likely one of the Campbell's. After slipping on my sandals, I follow her into the living room where Sadie is waiting.

"I see you have both been hard at work since yesterday," she says with a smile. The young woman is wearing a very revealing bikini top and cropped shorts. "I thought I would come by and see if you would like to take a walk through the neighborhood with me. There are some people in our community that I would love for you to meet."

"We would love to," Marcy replies as she nudges me. I get the feeling that she doesn't want me to continue ogling the other woman's chest so obviously. "Lead the way." Sadie turns and walks out our front door and we follow just behind her, my nose picking up on the trail of jasmine she is leaving in the air behind her.

As we begin our trip along the sidewalk, Sadie moves to my left side as Marcy steps to my right. The thought of being between the two attractive wives makes me just a little horny as my eyes occasionally look down at the neighbor's rack. My wife applies a nudge every so often to let me know that I'm being just a bit too obvious with my indiscriminate stares.

"This house belongs to Larry and Winnie Trevors," Sadie says as she waves a hand toward the home. "They're both attorneys in their own law firm. It's not often that they are here during the day, but they're definitely very active in our nightlife." She smiles and continues along the sidewalk.

"Next up is a wonderful couple." Sadie smiles and turns to take us toward the back of the house. "I think Renee should be back here this morning." As we round the corner of the house, I see a topless woman lying face-up on a lawn chair. "Renee!"

The woman turns to see us and then sits up on her chair. I'm surprised as she doesn't try to hide her breasts as we all three approach her short fence. There appears to be no shyness at all in her as she gets up and walks toward us.

"Don't," I hear Marcy say to me in a whisper to my side. I'm guessing that I'm staring once again, but I can't help it. The attractive woman's breasts are on full display as she approaches.

"Renee, this is Marcy and Jake." Sadie smiles as she turns to look at us.

"It's a pleasure." She takes Marcy's hand and shakes it before turning to look at me. "Up here, big guy." She motions her hands from her chest to her face. Though I wasn't actually looking at Renee's breasts just now, she must be referencing the stare I had made just as she got up from her chair. I blush as I shake her hand.

"I'm sorry about my husband," Macy says with embarrassment. "He's a typical male."

"It's fine," Renee laughs. "I'm not ashamed of my body at all. In fact, I'm proud of it. Johnny bought me these." She reaches down and puts her hands under her round breasts. Moving them around, she tells us, "They were not much more than an A-cup originally, but now they're a full D. Nice, huh?" Renee smiles at me as she lifts an eyebrow.

"I'm sorry that I looked."

"It's fine. I'm really fond of these." The woman twirls a nipple-stud on one of her nipples. "They actually glow in the dark."

"Do they really?" Sadie reaches over the small fence and touches one of the studs. She moves one herself and says, "I've got to talk to my hubby about getting my nipples pierced." She then pulls one side of her bikini down and exposes her own large, pink nipple. "I think maybe that would be fun."

"It definitely would be," Renee replies with a smile.

"Um, not me," Marcy says nervously. She's stopped nudging me now, most likely because she understands at last that there's just no way to avoid either one of us looking at the nipples that are being flashed around here.

"It's not for everyone," Renee says with a smile. "By the way, will you both be coming to the party Saturday evening?"

"Party?"

"Yes, the party. We have a huge blowout every three months or so in the neighborhood. Only people in our little gated community are invited to attend, which means you are both certainly welcome." Sadie smiles widely as she puts her breast back into her bikini top.

"Well, um, maybe," my wife replies. There's a sense of dread in her voice as she begins to realize that we have neighbors who are a little more open with their bodies than what we have experienced before.

"I hope so," Renee replies. "I would love to have a dance with you," she tells me.

"Sure." It's all I can say as I smile in the direction of the woman.

"Let's continue the tour, shall we?" Sadie says as she pats me on the back. "We'll see you this weekend, Renee."

"I'll see you all there." She smiles before walking back to her lawn chair and sitting down.

"She's a lot of fun," Sadie mentions as we make our way back to the sidewalk. "But she can be really pushy. Just ignore her if you need to on Saturday."

"Pushy in what way?" Marcy asks with concern.

Sadie shrugs her shoulders. "She's just one of those neighbors who are too friendly sometimes. I've had to ignore phone calls from her occasionally, but she means well. She will make a great friend if you can stand the way she will want to cling to you." Sadie smiles as she points out the next house. "Lola and Melanie live here. The nicest lesbian couple you will ever meet."

"Oh, really?" I say with some interest.

"Jake, don't," Marcy says as she once again nudges me.

Sadie laughs. "Luke is the same way. Men are men, am I right?"

"Yeah, you're right," my wife says as she looks hard at me. Though she has no proof that I had anything close to a sexual thought about the lesbians in the house, she knows me well enough to know that I like the idea of that sort of thing. I've always wanted to have a threesome with a pair of lesbian lovers.

We continue walking as Sadie tells us, "Our community events are a great way to make friends here. I want to encourage you both to come on Saturday evening to my home for this party. You'll have a great time."

"It's at your home?" Marcy asks.

"This time," Sadie replies. "We move the location each time. Who knows, maybe you will be ready to let us use your home in a few months for one of the next parties?"

"Maybe." Though my wife is looking forward to meeting new people, she doesn't like hosting parties all that much.

"It's at our home this time, though, so be sure to come and be a part of it. You'll love it." Sadie continues to guide us through the neighborhood, stopping at the occasional home to introduce us to another couple. Although we don't come across anyone quite like Renee as we make our way around, we do notice that some people are very scantily clad compared to what we would have experienced back in Boston. Of course, it is much warmer in Miami than in Boston this time of year, so I can see why some of them feel the need to air things out a bit more.

As we walk back to the front of our house, Sadie turns and asks, "So, what do you think? Is this the neighborhood for you, or what?" She smiles as she looks from one of us to the other.

"It's a very nice neighborhood," I reply. "Very nice."

"Because of Renee," Marcy says with a smirk on her face. She turns and looks at Sadie to add, "We like it here very much and look forward to getting to know people at the party on Saturday."

"So, you're coming?" My wife nods her head. "Yay!" Sadie walks up to Marcy and gives her a tight hug before doing the same to me. She pulls me close to her and the aroma of Jasmine once again strikes my nostrils, causing an embarrassing reaction. Sadie pulls back and pats my crotch. "Down boy." She laughs as she winks at Marcy. "Your hubby will need help with that in a minute." Barely pausing to look at my growing bulge, she then says, "Luke and I look forward to seeing the two of you on Saturday. Just come right in at around seven that evening, alright?"

"We'll be there." Marcy looks hard at me before smiling at our neighbor.

"I'll see the three of you later," Sadie says before taking one last look at my crotch then turning to walk away.

"The *three* of you," my wife says with embarrassment as she walks back to our house. "Honestly, Jake, can't you control yourself?"

"I didn't do it on purpose," I tell her while following close behind Marcy. She opens the door and we walk inside. "It just happened."

"And it just happened when you saw Renee too, huh?" My wife's accusatory expression concerns me as I shake my head and continue to try to defend myself.

"You have to understand that this was all just out of the ordinary for me, Marcy. I didn't get hard just to get hard. You saw what happened during that walk with her."

"I saw the boobs, yes, Jake. They were just boobs."

"For a guy, it's never just boobs, honey," I say with a smirk on my face. "You know that she was flirting with me. She didn't even attempt to cover herself."

"She's probably a nudist, Jake. Some people are just like that. You can't go around the neighborhood with a hardon whenever you see a topless woman." Marcy sighs. "I can't believe we have a woman nearby who doesn't mind talking about her nipple studs while showing them off to people."

I smile. "Maybe you should do that? A little topless sunbathing couldn't be too terrible, right?"

Marcy shakes her head. "There's no way that I will ever do that, Jake. Renee might be fine with it, but I'm not." She looks down at my crotch. "Can't you get that to go down or something?"

"You didn't complain about Luke's stuffed pants."

"He didn't have a hardon, though. It was just that his shorts were a little too tight, Jake. Right now you're hard because you can't stop thinking about Sadie and her friend Renee."

Shaking my head, I reply, "You know that wasn't my fault. Don't paint this as being all on me, honey. It's obvious that we have some freaky neighbors, so we're going to have to get used to it."

"And stop staring," she again says. "You are going to need to stop that. It's embarrassing, Jake. Just look at something else when you see that."

"Yeah, I'll do that. Just as soon as Sadie quits whipping her tits out in front of me." Marcy tries to return a stern expression, but she can't. We begin to laugh about what we have seen over the last two days in our new gated community. There are some odd people here, but that's fine. It's what will make our new home just a little different from anywhere we have stayed before.

"Please promise to behave yourself, alright? Even though our neighbors seem to be set on showing off a little around here, you shouldn't be too quick to take a look at them. Even Renee seemed to notice how interested you were in her breasts."

"She had them out. I didn't have to look all that hard to see them. Honestly, I think she *wants* people to look at them." My cock flexes a little as I think of the attractive young woman's assets as I shake my head. "There's something weird about this place, Marcy. I'm telling you, we are probably going to see a lot more T & A around here soon."

"It's Miami," she says flatly. "There's a lot of it around already. Just pretend you don't see it and try not to stare." Marcy walks up to me and taps my crotch in the same way Sadie did before winking at me and giggling. She turns to walk to our bedroom and I follow just behind. It doesn't take much more of a hint to let me know when I'm wanted. Whether that hint is from my wife or from someone else.

Chapter Three: Questions and Concerns

It's been a week since we have spoken to Dave and Cynthia Portman in Boston. They have been friends of ours for about five years and both Marcy and I miss them terribly. So, when my wife had the idea to FaceTime with them this evening, I was happy to do so with her. After all, it would be nice to see two familiar faces after the experiences we have had in our new home so far.

"Hey, guys," Cynthia says in her usual cadence as she waves at us from the other end of the FaceTime video call. "How are the two of you doing?" Dave sits down beside his wife and smiles at us as he lifts a cup of coffee in salute.

"We're doing okay. How have you been?" Marcy replies as she puts a hand on my knee. She's happy to see our old friends and I'm glad to see her so happy.

"We're good here too," she replies. "Boston is still Boston," Cynthia tells us, "But it's not the same without the two of you."

"We miss the both of you," Dave adds as he nods his head and smiles. "I'll bet it's warmer down there, huh?"

"Much warmer," I tell him. "And a little stranger too."

"Stranger?"

"Well, it's not what we are used to," Marcy offers as she attempts to erase their confusion. "The people here are a very open and welcoming sort. As a matter of fact, it seems as if clothing is optional for some of them."

"Ah, nudies?" Dave laughs as he shakes his head. "I could have told you there are some nudies around Miami. I've been there before."

"I think the term is *nudists,* sweetie," Cynthia corrects her husband while patting his knee. "And they didn't move into a nudist community. It's a gated community."

"I don't know..." I stop short of continuing as my own wife squeezes my knee. It appears to be one of the universal ways in which women control their talkative husbands.

"The neighbors are really nice, but some of them do things like sunbathe topless in their backyards. We've had one experience so far."

"And she didn't care that we could see her topless," I add.

"Geez, dude, did you get any pics? You know you can text them to me, right, buddy?"

"Will you just settle down?" Cynthia laughs as she shakes her head at her husband. "He's a little full of himself right now. He had a little too much to drink for dinner tonight."

Marcy looks at me and raises an eyebrow before replying, "Husbands are sometimes cut from the same cloth, Cynthia." The two women laugh as we two hubbies look at each other on our respective screens.

"When people put themselves out there nude, others are going to see them. There's no way to hide what's not already hidden unless you force them to hide it. It's an adult gated community, though, so the police don't patrol here. It's just the private security company that patrols."

"Does everyone there walk around naked?" Dave asks. It's apparent that he's about as interested in all this as I was in Renee's ample boobs.

"No, not everyone, though some of them might as well be. Our neighbor Sadie didn't have a bra on when she came to welcome us to the neighborhood with her husband the other day. And her husband had something going on in his pants."

"Socks," I say, to which Dave nods his understanding and laughs.

"That bulge was not due to socks, Jake. You know that." The wives seem just as interested in discussing Luke's large snake as Dave and I are in discussing Renee's two chest mountains. However, we quickly move on from this in order to avoid saying something too embarrassing.

"So, the job," Dave says. "When do you start, Jake?"

"In a week or so," I reply. "They are still getting all of the paperwork filled out for me to sign. It's a process and they told me to be prepared to wait as long as another two weeks."

"You're getting paid, though, right?"

Nodding my head, I reply, "Yeah, I'm getting my paychecks. It's giving the two of us time to look around the neighborhood and to enjoy the beach a little."

"Ah, the beach," Cynthia says with a smile. "I wish I was there with you, Marcy. We would have a great time on the beach together."

"Yeah, we would." The two wives giggle with each other. "Swimming and laying out all day sounds like fun to me. Jake and I haven't ventured out that far yet. There's still a lot to do to get things fixed up around the house."

"I'll bet there is," Cynthia replies. "Should we come down there to help you get things sorted out? "Dave and I have some time we can take off from work if we need to. We would be happy to do it."

"No, we're fine," my wife replies. "Jake and I have everything in hand for now. But, once we get things put away, it would be nice if the two of you could come visit for a few days. We could show you around Miami and hit the beach at that time."

"Sounds fun," she replies.

"And see some of the native wildlife in their neighborhood," Dave chuckles.

"Okay, I think that alcohol is going to his head now, guys. We should get off here and make him a little coffee to clear things up for him." Cynthia shakes her head as she looks over at her husband. He's obviously excited about what we've told them so far about the community we have just moved into.

"We'll see you both later," Dave says as he holds up a coffee mug. "More coffee for me." He stands up and walks out of the frame of the video.

"Stay away from the bottle of Jack, sweetie," his wife warns as she looks off-camera and shakes her head. "I've got to go make sure he's getting coffee only. Kisses to you both." Cynthia gives air kisses to us both and Marcy does the same before we log out of the FaceTime video.

I smile to myself as I think about how much of a handful our old neighbors can be whenever Dave has a bit too much to drink.

"What will she ever do with him?" Marcy laughs. "I'm glad you don't drink as much as Dave does."

"I'm really not big on alcohol," I reply. "I'm more of the type that prefers to enjoy things without being drunk or high."

"That's a good thing." My wife reaches over and pats my knee. There's a look on her face that causes me to feel concerned for her.

"What's wrong?" I ask.

She shakes her head. "Nothing, really. I'm just thinking about how I miss the two of them and the other people we left behind in Boston. Do you think we made a mistake by moving, Jake?"

"A mistake? By moving?" Marcy nods her head. "No, I don't think we made a mistake, honey. This new position pays *double* what the old one did, remember? That's why we can afford to live in a gated community in the first place."

"I know," she replies. "Still, things here aren't what I expected them to be when we left Boston. I thought we would get to enjoy the ocean every afternoon, but so far we've only been there a couple of times." Marcy sighs. "I don't mean to complain, but this place is not what I had expected."

"Ah," I say while nodding my head. "You don't like what you've seen so far around here. The whole thing with Sadie, Luke, and Renee still bothers you."

Her green eyes turn to meet mine. "Don't they make you just a little nervous, Jake? They showed off a lot before they really even knew the two of us. Who does that?"

"I don't know," I reply. "Maybe that's just their way. We talked about that yesterday, remember? They are probably just a little more eccentric than what we are used to dealing with back in Boston. Keep in mind that most of the people who live here don't have to work anymore, baby. They are wealthy and they have others who run their businesses for the most part."

"Except for the attorneys down the street," Marcy answers. "They are apparently gone all the time."

I nod my head. "And that's just one indicator that this area isn't as weird as you think it is." I reach out and take Marcy's hand into mine. "You miss Cynthia and your other friends, but we'll make new ones here. Sure, we will have to have them over for visits, but for now our old friends are not in our lives. It's time for us to do what we can to make things more comfortable for us, right? Just give it time, honey." Leaning over, I give my wife a quick kiss on the cheek. She smiles, but I can see the hurt that is still inside her. There's not much I can do about that as I pat her knee. "There's that party this weekend too, remember? That's supposedly going to be a great time for us all."

"Yeah, maybe." Marcy sighs. "I hope Renee will find a top to wear before she comes to the party, though. It wouldn't look good if my husband ends up staring at another woman's chest at the party." She smiles smugly at me.

"Hey, if she shows up to the party without her top on, there will be *lots* of other men looking at her as well. It wouldn't just be me."

"Just try to control yourself, Jake. Be a good boy." Marcy returns to kiss my cheek before getting up from the sofa. "I'm going to get me a glass of water. Would you like something as well?"

"Sure. I'll take a soft drink," I tell her as I watch my wife walk out of the room. Turning my attention to the window nearby, I watch as Sadie works on the flowers on her front porch. Her outfit today involves a very small tied-up tee shirt that has been cut on the bottom to reveal her physically fit midriff. There's no denying that the woman next door is highly attractive and very sexual in the way she presents herself to others. Just yesterday she felt my growing hardon as I hugged her tightly. It's possible that I had something to do with making certain that she would feel it, but even so, she reached out to confirm with her hand that I was hard. All in front of my wife. That was a ballsy move for her, as well as for me.

As I take the glass of water from Marcy, I sit back and think about what we have seen and heard over the last couple of days in our new neighborhood. Things are definitely not the same around here as they were in Boston, but a lot of that was to be expected in a place like Miami. The greeting we have received from our neighbors, though, was not. Hopefully the party this weekend will help to settle some questions that Marcy and I have about our new home and the community we find ourselves in.

Chapter Four: Not Just Any Party

The music is loud as we walk into our neighbors' house next door. There appear to be more than two dozen people in the large living room and dining room, all of them dancing, drinking, or doing a combination of both. Luke and Sadie Campbell walk over to welcome us into their home.

"Hello! We're so glad you could make it," Luke says to us as he reaches out to pat me on the side of the arm. The two ladies hug each other before we then exchange partners to greet each other. I'm a little surprised as Sadie's lips graze the side of my face and her hand runs along the lower part of my back. It's not that I'm repulsed at all by her greeting, but I can't remember a time when the wife of another man has intentionally been so affectionate to me.

"We have lots to show you tonight," Sadie says with a smile on her face as she backs away from me and smiles at us both. "You're in for a great time!"

"What sort of party is this again?" my wife asks.

"We call it a key club party," Luke replies. "As a matter of fact, we need a copy of your house key, Jake." He looks at me as if this is some sort of normal request.

"My house key? Why?"

"Just play along," Sadie answers with a smile. "We play a game using our house keys. Don't worry, you'll get it back." The young woman watches me closely as I reach into my pocket and pull out my house key. I hand it over to Luke and he immediately places it into a small, plain envelope. "You're number one-sixty-seven," he tells me.

"The same as our address?" I reply.

"Yes, the same. It's how this game is played, with a key and an address." Luke looks over at Sadie and tells her, "I'm going to go put this with the others. We'll be drawing soon."

"The sooner the better." His wife nods at him and then watches as he walks away. "It was his idea."

"The game?" Marcy asks.

Sadie nods her head. "The whole party thing and the keys game. After a while, we started referring to this as the key club because of the way everyone on the street wanted to be a part of this. Only the most prominent of our little gated community attend."

"Really? Prominent?" I chuckle. "We just got here."

"Still, I like the both of you," she tells me. "You both seem to fit in here very well and so I am hoping that you will have a lot of fun tonight. I would be willing to bet everything I have that you will." A sort of devilish grin appears on Sadie's face. There's something about this party that is not what most people would expect. For one thing, I can see that some people are making their way around the room and flirting with others. That's not something you often see when couples attend parties together, but who am I to judge?

"We like games," Marcy says as she nods her head at our host. "I'm sure we will have a great time."

"You will." Sadie turns to leave, but as she does, she winks at me. I feel goosebumps form on the back of my neck as I watch the young wife leave Marcy and I alone. I have the distinct feeling that there is some sort of surprise awaiting us.

"I wonder what they're up to," I say out loud.

"It's a game," my wife replies. "I'm sure they'll fill us in on the rules soon." Turning her attention to the others at the party, Marcy adds, "I think we should make our way around the room and introduce ourselves. We haven't met all of our neighbors yet." She turns and walks away from me as I wonder whether I should go along with her. Something stops me as I look around the room and recognize some of the people we have already met. Everyone is dressed this time, but their clothing is definitely revealing and sexually suspect. Why is it that people in our little gated community feel the need to dress so provocatively? Is it just a community norm that most of them adhere to without much thought? Somehow, I doubt it. There is a purpose to their attire, I'm certain of it.

After another half-hour and a couple of drinks, I hear Luke Campbell call out to get our attention. "Everybody, please," he says after ringing a small bell. "Listen up. We are ready for the game." The others in the large living room become still as they turn and look at the handsome man. "As many of you know, we have a new couple in our community." Waving his hand toward my wife, he says, "This is Marcy, who lives next door to us." The party guests clap their hands as they look in her direction.

Luke's eyes then scan the room until he finds me. "And her lesser half..." Everyone laughs as they turn their attention to me at the direction of his hand. "Marcy's husband, Jake." Clapping follows the laughter as I feel my face flood with red. My wife smiles at me before turning her attention back to our host.

"The rules of the game are quite clear," he begins as he reaches down for a small woven basket on a table next to him. "The keys from the men in this room are inside. The ladies will each draw a key from the basket. Once you do, you will look at the address on the tag attached to the key. That is where you ladies will be going." Luke looks around the room and continues, "You men will go home after the drawing without knowing which woman is coming to your house. When she gets there, she will knock on the front door and you will let her inside. For the rest of the night, you will stay in your house together. It would be a good time to get to know each other and talk about each other's spouses." A wicked smile crosses his face. "Of course, whatever else happens, happens. There will be no discussion with your wife or husband about what is said or done tonight. Is that clear?" Most of the men and women in the room raise their glasses or say something like 'clear' to answer our host. My skin begins to prickle even more as the obvious fills my mind.

"So, ladies, are you ready?" Sadie walks up and reaches into the basket. "Remember, if you get your own key you need to trade it into the basket for another. This is an icebreaker game."

"Gentlemen, it's time for you to go home." I'm still a little confused as I watch the men in the room begin to walk toward the front door. Luke walks up to me with a smile on his face. "It's going to be okay, Jake."

"I'm locked out of my house," I joke nervously. "I don't have a key." I look at the basket at the front of the room where the women are drawing for keys.

"Oh, yeah." He reaches into his pocket and fishes out a key. "Sadie got this from Marcy. I think there might have been some confusion earlier about the keys. Besides, most of us leave our doors unlocked on this night."

"But..."

"Gated, well-guarded community," he interrupts. "Go ahead. Someone will be at your house soon, Jake." Luke smiles as he walks me to the door. Without saying another word, I leave the house and the door closes behind me.

"Um...what the fuck?" I begin to walk toward my house while trying to sort out what has just happened. Though I want to believe that Marcy is safe, I begin to question just what might be happening to her inside the house. She's still there, and I'm now out here walking along the sidewalk a short distance to our home. If it wasn't for the fact that the other men at the party are leaving as well, I would be very inclined to go back inside to retrieve my wife.

After I get inside my house, I find myself having a great deal of difficulty settling down to wait for whatever is going to happen. Pacing the floor, I begin to talk to myself as I reason what is going on. "Is this a cult?" I wonder. "Maybe some kind of weird initiation for new people in the neighborhood? What the fuck do they mean when they say the women are drawing keys and going to other homes?" My heart races as I begin to answer my own questions. A cult? Likely not, but still, something weird is going on around here. An initiation? No. I don't think so. However, the drawing of keys was definitely taking place. All I know is that someone else besides my wife is supposed to come here and I'm supposed to let her in.

I jump as there is a slight knock on the front door. After walking to the door, I open it to find Sadie standing on the other side. She smiles, says nothing at first, and walks into my home. Closing the door, I struggle to control the thoughts racing through my mind.

"Hello, Jake," she says with a smile as she looks around the living room. "You and Marcy have done a lot around here since I last saw this place."

"Yeah." Sadie is wearing a tight tee shirt with no bra as well as a pair of jeans that are tight and revealing. After swallowing hard, I ask, "So, what is this game, really?"

She smiles. "The game is this." Sadie walks up to me and while looking into my eyes she runs her fingers along my chest. "We just get to know each other." She then turns and walks over to the sofa. Patting the cushion beside her, she waits for me to join her.

As I sit down, I ask, "Where's Marcy?"

Sadie shrugs her shoulders. "I don't know. She left when I did. I would guess that she's at the house that matches her key."

I shake my head. "Did you really draw the key to this house?"

"Of course I did, silly." She smiles as she pulls back her shoulder-length dark brown hair. "Are you nervous, Jake? You seem very nervous."

"I don't know. Should I be?" I ask as my voice cracks a little. "Seriously, what's this all about? Everything seems so secretive."

"Nothing's a secret," she answers. "You know what this is about, Jake. All you have to do is admit it to yourself."

My eyes widen. "You don't mean that. You're just trying to see what I will do. I'm a faithful husband, Sadie. Marcy is faithful to me, too."

"Faithfulness has nothing to do with this," she replies as she reaches down and begins to unfasten my pants. "It has to do with getting to know your neighbors better. That's all it is. You and Marcy will continue to be husband and wife throughout this little game and afterward. Remember, it's *just* a game." Sadie finds my cock and pulls it out through the opening in my pants, causing it to harden immediately inside her hand. Before I can respond, she kneels down on the floor in front of me and takes my manly meat into her mouth.

"*Shit*," I say breathlessly as she pushes my hard stalk all the way to the back of her throat. Sadie doesn't gag as she rams the solid head of it hard between her tonsils, causing me to buck a little on the sofa. "*Fuck.*"

Sadie sucks gently on me for a minute or so before lifting her head. Her hand continues to caress my hardness as she asks, "Do you like what I'm doing to you, Jake?"

"Marcy won't like this," I tell her. "I know my wife. She won't like this at all." I think for a moment about reaching down and pushing her hands away, but I don't. Instead, I allow her to continue to fondle my swollen cock.

"Part of this game is that you never tell her about what happens here tonight, Jake. Just as Marcy is to never tell you what happens tonight at the house where she has gone." Sadie allows a smile before going back down on me, her lips gripping the sides of my manhood tightly as she sucks even harder than before.

"Oh, damn, that's intense," I tell Luke's wife as she siphons my fleshy hose. "Marcy will be so angry." Sadie doesn't stop as I feel myself getting closer and closer to losing my wad. Why does she want to give me a blow job? Is there some attraction she has had for me since we met? Does Luke know what his wife is doing to me right now? "I'm going to come," I tell her as I feel my body tense. "If you don't want me to..." It's all I can say before the first spurt leaves my cock and floods the young woman's mouth. *Fuck...FUCK!!! OHHHH!!!*" Gritting my teeth, I think about the last time another woman besides my wife gave me a blow job. It's been more than ten years since Sharri Martin swallowed my spunk at the end of our second date. Though she was happy to give me head, we were over as a couple a little less than a week later. It was not long after that I met my future wife.

"*Uhhh...uhhh...ahhhh...*" I empty my balls into Sadie's mouth before finally coming down from my orgasm. She doesn't allow a single drop of my jism to be lost as she slurps hard and swallows all of it.

"Good?" She wipes her lips as she sits back on the sofa beside me. I quickly pull my softening penis back into my pants and nervously look over at her.

"Why? What does this have to do with a game?" I ask.

Sadie giggles. "You now know something about me, Jake. You know that I can give great blow jobs, right? Now, tell me, what is something that I don't know about you." She puts a hand on my lap as my body quivers from the after-effects of oral satisfaction.

"Nothing," I tell her, embarrassed at myself for allowing another woman to pleasure me. "I can't think of anything."

"Okay." Sadie looks over at a door to the master bedroom. "Let's go to bed, then."

"Bed?" I stare at the young woman beside me. "We can't do that. Marcy could be here at any time."

She shakes her head. "She won't be here until after eight in the morning. That's one of the rules," Luke's wife tells me. "She is supposed to stay where she's at until then. There's to be no wandering around and trying to figure out where each woman has been. Trust me, Jake, it's all going to be okay. Don't be like this." She gets up from the sofa and then holds a hand out to me. "Come with me. I promise; I won't bite."

"I don't know..."

"Jake. Come with me." Her dark brown eyes stare down at me as she waits for me to take her hand. I finally do as I get up from the sofa. We make our way to the bedroom and I quietly begin to wonder what is next. Will we be having full sex? Is this where she will find an ice pick and murder me while riding me hard? One thing I do know as we enter the master bedroom is that Sadie can give head better than anyone I've gotten head from before. That assessment includes my own wife, Marcy. I feel ashamed to admit as much to myself, but it is in complete honesty. Whatever she has planned in the bedroom for me, Sadie will likely be the best at it as well. This fact scares me as I worry about what Marcy is doing right now. I have to work to keep my mind off that thought. At least, for now.

Chapter Five: A Different Sort of Encounter

The whole morning has been quiet since Marcy came back home. Neither of us has said a word about what happened last night after the ladies drew for keys at the party. For my part, I'm embarrassed that I got a blow job from Sadie. What's even stranger is that she didn't push me for sex. She insisted that we sleep together while fully nude in bed, but nothing else sexual in nature happened outside of that. As a matter of fact, she cuddled up close to me, her perky breasts against my shoulder, and fell asleep. It was as if we were a married couple simply enjoying each other's presence. By the time I awoke this morning, she had already left my house.

"Jake," Marcy finally says quietly after taking a sip of coffee. "You know I love you, right? That will never change."

I nod my head. "I know that. And I love you too." I stop short of asking her anything about what happened between her and the other man she was with last night. It could have been fairly innocent. They might have just sat and talked to each other all night, though I have the feeling that it didn't stop with just that.

"Sadie was the one who came over," I blurt out suddenly. The declaration causes me to wince as Marcy looks over at me, surprise on her face.

"Sadie?"

"Yeah. I'm sorry." I take a sip of my own coffee as I ponder what my wife's response might be.

"Sadie," she says again while looking back down at her cup. "I think she might have set that part of the drawing up. She was talking about you a lot when I went with her before the drawing. She constantly asked questions about you and what you liked. Some of the conversation was even a little sexual." Marcy stops herself as she looks over at me. "Just tell me, Jake. Did you have sex with her?" Her green eyes focus on me as she awaits an answer.

"Honey," I begin as I avoid eye contact. "We didn't have sex." The answer is a bit misleading.

"Then what did you do?"

I shake my head. "First, whose house did you go to? Did you stay there with Luke?"

Marcy sighs. "No. I went to another house, Jake. It was a man named Dawson who met me there." She swallows hard as she glares at me. "Things did happen, though."

My heart beats hard as I ask, "What exactly happened, Marcy? Just tell me." Now I'm asking my wife to do the same as she asked me. We both want to know what went on in our respective roles in the key game. Still, will either of us be completely honest?"

"Did she give you a blow job?" my wife asks me. I shake as I begin to wonder if she has already spoken to Sadie.

"A blow job?"

"That's one of the things she asked me, Jake. She asked if you liked oral sex. I told her that you loved blow jobs. Did she give you one?" Marcy's eyes watch me closely as her expression changes. "She gave you a blow job, didn't she?"

"Honey..."

"She *did*. Sadie gave you a fucking blow job. Fuck." Marcy turns her face from me for a moment as she considers how I have cheated on her.

"Please don't be angry, baby. It wasn't like I was trying to get her to do something with me. Sadie came in here and she just did it. I didn't stop her, though. I know I should have, but..."

"I slept with him, Jake," my wife interrupts as she turns back to face me. The admission almost seems to be retribution for the fact that I allowed Sadie to mouth fuck me.

"What?"

She looks at me, her demeanor almost stern. "I had sex with Dawson. I even orgasmed twice."

"No." Frowning, I try to understand whether Marcy is being truthful with me or simply vengeful. Surely my wife of nearly ten years wouldn't actually screw another man. Right?

"He was powerful," she tells me softly. "It was something that I didn't expect, but he convinced me that we could do that, even though we are both married to other people. I told him that it wouldn't be right, but he insisted. One thing led to another, and then we had sex." Her green eyes look intently into mine. "I don't blame you for what happened between you and Sadie. It all makes sense now, though. That key thing they did is a community-wide game and they do it every three months or so, Jake. This is the way of life in this place."

"Fuck." I shake my head as I realize how far Marcy and I have strayed from the sorts of people we were when we first moved to this gated community less than a week ago. Before coming here, we were fully into each other and had a very active sex life. After what happened last night, though, I wonder if anything will ever be the same between us again.

"We need to talk to Sadie and Luke."

"Why?" I shake my head. "We aren't even supposed to tell each other what happened. They said it's one of the rules, Marcy."

"I don't give a shit about the rules," she replies as she picks up her cell phone. She finds a number in her contacts list and selects it. Her phone begins to dial the number as my wife puts it on speaker.

"What are you doing?"

"Calling them," she says with a grimace on her face. "I want to know the truth. I want to know exactly what we have moved into, Jake."

Sadie's voice suddenly comes across on the phone's speaker. "Hello?"

"Hey Sadie," my wife replies as she folds her arms and sits back in her seat at the dining room table. "This is Marcy."

"Good morning, Marcy," she answers. "Sleep well?"

"I slept fine," my wife says as she grimaces. "Jake and I have been talking. We need some answers."

"Answers?" There's a pause on the other end before Sadie continues, "You told each other, didn't you?"

"Of course they did," Luke chuckles on the other end of the line with her. "You knew they would."

"What? Did you set us up?" I ask.

"Set you up? What do you mean?" Sadie replies.

"He means that it seems odd that you came here to see him after talking to me," Marcy tells her. "Did you tilt the odds in your favor, Sadie? Did you hold onto that key for yourself?"

There is silence before Sadie replies, "Of course I did. Your husband is just so...tempting."

"Tempting?" I shake my head as I chuckle. "That's not the way I would look at myself."

"After last night I want you even more," she tells me. "You didn't try one time to fuck me, Jake. Why not?" My face turns red as I look down at the table in front of me. "You're a gentleman, that's why. You wanted to, though. You had a hardon all night long and you kept moaning in your sleep. I just wish you had let me take care of that for you in bed." Sadie giggles.

"And you had a good time with Dawson, right, Marcy?" Luke asks.

Marcy looks at me and then replies, "Is this really what happens at these key parties, or did you just do this to toy with us and our feelings?"

"Feelings? There are no feelings involved," Luke answers. "Marcy, this is a chance for neighbors to have a little fun with each other, no strings attached. Most of the people here in our little community never talk about what happened with their spouses. It helps to avoid any jealousies or other problems. We don't talk about what happens and we don't fall for the other person."

"But, I can't just *not* tell her," I reply. "Marcy is my wife and I love her, no matter what happened last night. We both made a mistake, but we love each other too much to let it tear us apart."

"Jake," Sadie begins. "We are not trying to tear anyone apart. This party is the opportunity for couples to experience something different in the safety of our gated community. This wasn't an orgy, right? It was just some time between two willing adults."

"Willing?"

"Willing," she reiterates. "You didn't turn me down, did you? Jake, you liked what I did to you, right?" Sadie giggles a little on the other end. She's enjoying talking about this in front of Marcy, no matter what she said to me about keeping what happened between us a secret.

"What now?" Marcy asks. Her face is pink as she looks across the table at me. "What do we do now that we have done this?" I'm not certain why my wife asks this question. Is she worried that from here on out our marriage will be marred with what happened last night?

"Now, you come see us," Sadie replies. "You both come see us and see what we are really about."

"Come see you? Why?" I don't know what to think about Sadie's reply to Marcy's concern.

There is silence on the other end of the line before Luke replies, "We want to get to know you better as a couple, Jake. It would just be the four of us."

"I don't know," Marcy begins as she shakes her head.

"Just dinner with us," Sadie says. "Nothing will happen without the understanding and agreement of both of you."

"But you're thinking of sex, aren't you?" I say daringly into the phone. "You want us to have sex with you both."

"Sex is always on the table," Sadie replies. "Luke and I never discount anything that might lead to sex. We are a very open couple, and if you're not, that's perfectly okay. We don't expect you to do anything that you don't want to do, Jake. Just come to dinner and we'll talk."

"When?" Marcy asks.

"Tonight."

My wife looks at me, her expression of concern matching my own. We have already had extramarital relations with others. What will happen if we walk back into our neighbors' home where the party began last night? Will we end up having sex or getting something orally from them? Will they expect us to do something to repay whatever they think they have done for us since coming to the neighborhood? The cult idea is still fresh in my mind and I'm worried that the Campbell's might be trying to gain control of us through sex.

"Tonight," Marcy finally answers. "Seven?"

"That will be fine," Luke replies. "Surf and turf, if that's alright."

"Oh, you are both in for a treat," Sadie laughs. "My hubby is great at making both lobster and steak."

"We'll be there," Marcy tells her. "And we'll just talk. I have lots of questions for both of you."

"I know you do, dear," the other wife replies. "We'll see you this evening." They hang up the phone on their side and we are left to look questioningly at each other.

"This is probably not the best idea," I tell her. "They have already said that they would like to have sex with us."

"I know," she replies. "And we'll just have to resist whatever they try on us. I want to know what is really going on here, Jake. It's obvious that Luke and Sadie are the two people who know the most around the community. They are the ones pushing things around here."

I nod my head. "Maybe they are. Sadie will try something on me, though. I know she will."

"She won't. Not with me there," Marcy answers with conviction. "We will keep each other faithful." She smiles uneasily at me before finishing her coffee. My wife wants to know more about the key club and why they do it. If this happens every three months and we plan to stick around, we'll want to know what is really going on. Is there some sort of control being enacted throughout the neighborhood? Whatever it is, we will have questions tonight as we eat at the neighbors' house.

Chapter Six: Admission of Desires

"Come in!" Sadie smiles as she welcomes us through the front door of their home. Luke is waiting just inside, holding a small glass of scotch whiskey in his hand. "Can I get you something to drink?"

"I'll have what he's having," I say with a nervous chuckle. The fact is, I will probably need a little liquid courage while talking to the Campbell's tonight. After what Sadie did to me at our house, I can't really look at her the same way again.

"Some wine, maybe?" Marcy smiles at Sadie, though I can see by the expression on her face that she's thinking about the other woman's lips on my pecker just last night. Though this get-together is odd enough for me, I'm sure it's completely weird for her.

"Scotch and wine. I'll get those for you both right away." Sadie smiles and nods before walking away and leaving us with the man of the house.

"Please, have a seat," Luke says while waving his hand in the direction of the sofa. We sit down and he continues. "I'll bet you both have a million questions about the party last night, huh?" His eyes sparkle as he looks from me to my wife. "It was a little different than anything you've done before, right?"

Swallowing hard, I reply, "I think that's probably a huge understatement." I find it extremely difficult to look the man in the eyes. His wife did, after all, siphon me until I was dry.

"It's a little daunting at first, but you will soon get used to it. You even get to the point where you look forward to it." Luke smiles before taking another drink of his scotch. He has one leg propped over the other, his foot wagging just to the side of his knee as he looks at my wife. "I'm sorry that you didn't draw my key."

"I'll bet you are," Sadie laughs as she walks back into the living room with our drinks. She walks over to Marcy and gives her a glass of red wine before making her way to me to deliver a glass of whiskey. "It has been all Luke has been able to talk about all day long. I don't think Janine was really his type."

"She's a lovely woman, but she doesn't have the experience that most women have. Janine is nearly forty years old and yet she can't really give a proper blow job."

"Sweetie, don't share," Sadie scolds. "You know the rules. We're supposed to keep that stuff to ourselves." The beautiful wife then turns to look at me. "I know you think that I've told Luke about our little rendezvous, but I honestly haven't. What happened is between just the two of us." She reaches over to a small table near her chair and picks up a glass of wine. After taking a drink, she nods at Marcy and adds, "I hope you aren't angry with me for drawing Jake's key."

Marcy looks for a moment at me and then at Sadie. "We talked about what happened. I know we're not supposed to, but we're married, so..."

"You felt compelled to confess and ask forgiveness," Luke muses. "That happens the first time or two, but you get used to it all and soon you don't expect information from your spouse."

"Unless you decide to brag." Sadie allows a wry look at her husband. "Besides, you come to realize that what defines you as a couple is just between the two of you. It really has nothing to do with what you do with other people. Honestly, it's just sex. The sex is between neighbors who are both safe and welcoming."

My body shakes a little as I cradle the glass of whiskey in my hands. "Did you rig the drawing so that you could come to my house?" I ask her. It's something I wondered while Sadie was giving me oral satisfaction last night. The theory seems to make sense, though it very well might have been a coincidence.

Sadie grins wickedly. "I can't tell you exactly how I came to have your house key, Jake, but I did cheat just a little to get it. That's what matters, right?" There's no question in my mind that she wanted to come to my house. Luke's wife has all but admitted as much.

"I have an idea," Luke says with a wicked smile. "What if we all get more comfortable? Wouldn't that be nice?" He stands up after putting his whiskey down and then lifts his tee shirt over his heat. His rippling chest is a feast for my wife's eyes as she looks hard at him. The other man smiles at her as he then pulls down his pants and reveals a growing erection. A very *large* growing erection.

"Sweetie, you're pushy. Do you know that?" Sadie giggles as she watches her husband have a seat and then stroke his hard pole. Looking toward us, she asks, "Would it bother you?" She doesn't wait for an answer before she stands up and sheds her clothing as well. I didn't get the chance to see Sadie's beautiful body before, but now I can see her beautiful, full breasts and nicely trimmed muff. My own cock stiffens as I stand to my feet to take off my clothes as well.

"Jake," Marcy whispers. I pretend not to hear her as I show off my erect phallus to the Campbell's

"Come on, Marcy. You can do this." Sadie sits down on a chair and puts her legs up over the arms of it. Her fingers make their way down to her soft pussy before they disappear into her wet hole. I groan a little as I pull on my manhood.

"Please, Marcy." Luke waves my wife over to him. She goes over and he reaches out for her hand. After taking it into his own hands, he pulls it down to his hard shaft and wraps it around it. "Your hand is so soft," he tells her as my wife begins to give him a soft hand job. "So fucking soft." Luke spreads his legs and relaxes as she puts her other hand on him and begins to jerk a little faster. Though Marcy appears at first to protest this, she seems to begin to enjoy playing with his cock.

I move toward Sadie as she continues to play with herself. The aroma of pussy is in the air as she pulls more and more of her natural lubrication out to smear over her swelling clitoris. Luke's wife smiles at me as I kneel down on the floor between her legs. She allows her feet to rest on my shoulders as I go down and begin to taste her sweet twat.

"*Jake...*" Sadie is breathless as I begin to run my tongue around her clit and then down between her folds. Her juices are sweet and delightful to my mouth as I enjoy eating her out. "Shit, Jake. That's it...oh, *fuck.*" Her hands go to her large, pink nipples where her fingers pinch and pull on each one. The petite woman's body shudders as she squirms around in the chair as I lick and nip at every part of her beaver.

"Squeeze my balls," I hear Luke tell Marcy. "That's the way. Just gently squeeze them." He pauses before asking, "Can you suck on it? Please?" I lift my head to look over at them for a moment. To my surprise, Marcy opens her mouth and takes the other man's cock in. *"Holy shit..."* He leans back and just enjoys my wife's sweet mouth running up and down his long, hard shaft. I get even harder thinking about him coming inside her throat as I go back down on Sadie.

"You're a natural," Sadie tells me as I continue to feast upon her muffin. "Finger me, Jake." I do as she asks and reach up to insert two of my fingers into her pussy. I curl them and run them against her soft bump at the front of her vagina. Sadie's small body reacts wildly as I stroke her G-spot over and over again. "Jake...oh, Jake..." Her fingers move through my hair as she grinds her pussy into my face. "You're going to make me come soon."

"Oh...*ahhhhh*..." Luke begins to spurt as Marcy's mouth seats tightly on his pecker. *"Ahhh...uhhh...uhhh...uhhh..."* Each burst of semen must be powerful as I hear my wife gag several times while catching his thick spunk in the back of her throat.

"ACK!!! UTTTT!!!" Marcy isn't the greatest at swallowing, but I would put her oral skills against anyone. She doesn't vomit or spit out the man gravy filling her mouth. My wife swallows every bit of Luke's come as he delivers it to her.

"GAWWWWW!!!" Sadie grips my hair tightly and pulls my face hard into her musky pudding. *"OHHHHH!!!"* She shrieks loudly as she orgasms and covers my face in her pussy juices. Sweet and light, I lap at them and consume as much of them as I can while she comes. *"JAKE! FUCK!!!"* The chair moves around on the floor as her small body wags back and forth in it. Marcy has had some pretty intense orgasms with me in the past, but I can't recall any that were as intense as what Sadie is having at this moment with me. *"Ohhhh..."*

In the next few moments, Sadie's body relaxes and her legs rest fully on my shoulders. She's finished. I lift my head and ask, "Was that alright?"

Her hands laying over her breasts as she breathes deeply, Luke's wife looks down at me and replies, "That was the best orgasm I've had in a very long time."

"Oh, come on, dear," Luke laughs as he looks over at his wife.

I sit up and look over at Marcy. Luke's spunk is all over her face as she tries to wipe it off with the hem of her tee shirt. She is the only one who has managed to keep her clothes on during this.

"Would you both like to trade places?" Sadie asks. "We sort of owe you now."

Marcy shakes her head. "No, we need to go."

"But, dinner," I say to her. "We came for that."

"I think maybe I've overdone the appetizer for her," Luke chuckles.

"Let's just go, alright? I just want to get home and take care of some things I need to do."

"Have we said or done something to upset you?" Sadie asks as she sits up in her chair, her wetness covering the top of the cushion.

"No, this was all fine," Marcy says with a half-smile. "I enjoyed it. I really did. It's just that I've remembered there is something I should have already taken care of and I need to do that as soon as I can." Looking at me, my wife tells me, "You can stay here if you would like. I just need to go." Marcy stands up and goes to the door. I reach down and pick up my clothes, putting them on as quickly as I can.

"Is she okay?" Sadie asks as concern fills her face. She stands to her feet and begins to get dressed as well. "Maybe we shouldn't have done this so soon."

"She's fine," I reply as I smile at her. "Marcy can just get a little overwhelmed sometimes, that's all. I should go with her, though. Otherwise, she might get upset with me later."

"Understood." Luke pats me on the shoulder, his spent cock still dangling freely for all to see. "Let us know if there is anything we can do. Honestly, we didn't want to do anything to upset either of you."

"We're fine. I'll talk to you later." With that, I go to meet Marcy at the door. We leave the house and make our way back home. There is obviously something about this encounter that has bothered my beautiful wife, and I want to find out what it is. The last thing I want is to do anything that could break down our marriage.

Chapter Seven: Dangerous Guilt

"Honey, are you alright?" I close the door and then make my way to where Marcy is staring out the front window of our home.

"I'm sorry that I got that way," she replies quietly. "I just couldn't stay in there any longer." My wife swallows hard as she runs a hand around her neck. "I don't know that what we are doing is a good idea, Jake. This might hurt our marriage eventually."

"What?" I shake my head. "You know that I only love you, right? This was only about sex, baby. There's nothing else to what happened tonight or last night. It was all just sex between adults."

"With *her.*" Marcy looks hard at me. "She *likes* you, Jake. That woman wants you more than she wants her own husband."

I shake my head. "I don't think that's true. Marcy, she's just a very sexual person, that's all."

"For *you.*" The accusatory tone in my wife's voice grows stronger as she continues to glare at me. "She fixed that key basket, Jake, by her own admission. If that's not enough evidence for you, then just think about how she orgasmed with you. She said that it was the best she's had in a long time. She said it in front of her husband!" Marcy shakes her head and turns to begin pacing the floor slowly. *"Fuck her."*

"Honey..."

"Sadie is going to take you away from me," my wife continues. "You can see that could happen, right? I mean, you liked it too, didn't you?" Marcy's face is drawn as she looks at me now. Her expression has gone from accusatory to resigned. My wife really does seem to believe that Sadie is trying to take me away from her.

"Look, Marcy," I say as I put a hand on her shoulder. "You're reading too much into this. The entire community here has become an adult community. You've noticed that there are no children here, haven't you? They don't look for people to buy into this area unless they are free of such things. All that is going on here is the neighborhood is having a lot of sex. We are having sex with others. You had sex with another man last

evening. Didn't you like it?" My wife's eyes turn from me for a moment
as she recalls her time with him.

"I liked it," she admits. "But then again, you weren't watching me
with him. Tonight, though, I could see you eating her out. Sadie *really*
liked it."

"And Luke enjoyed coming inside your mouth, honey. You're not
normally the type to swallow the way that you did. With me, you usually
catch it all in your mouth and then spit. You swallowed his jism."

"Doesn't that bother you a little?" she asks while shaking her head.
"Jake, I'm terrible. I know what you want here and I have to confess that
I want to screw around too. But, when I saw you with her..." She turns
from me again.

"That's what this is all about, then. Honey, you don't like to see me
with another woman, do you?"

"No, I don't," she agrees. "But there you were, eating her pussy."
Marcy scrunches her nose as she turns back to face me. "I wanted to beat
the hell out of Sadie after she finished coming. I know that doesn't make
any sense, but I did."

I laugh. "I know what you mean. To be perfectly honest, when you
went to someone else's house without me, that bothered me even more.
Having you in the same room made things easier for me. It seems that we
are wired a little differently, huh?"

Marcy giggles a little. "I guess we are." She comes closer to me and
puts her arms around my neck. I can smell Luke's spunk still on her
breath. "You want to keep doing this, don't you?"

"I would like to," I tell her, "But I would never do anything that
would make you too uncomfortable, my love. It wouldn't be worth
having sex with other people if you aren't willing to go along for the ride."
After kissing her on the forehead, I ask Marcy, "Do you want to keep
trying for now, or should I look into getting us moved somewhere else.
After all, there's really no sense in being her if we aren't going to be a real
part of this community."

She sighs. "I want to try to make things work here, Jake. I know you want it and so do I. There's something a little freeing about spending time with another person." Her face blushes. "What did you think about when you saw me sucking on Luke's dick?"

Smiling, I reply, "Well, it turned me on a lot. It got me very hard."

"Did it make you want to fuck Sadie?" Marcy asks. "You didn't get to fuck her the other night, right? She just gave you a blow job."

I nod my head. "You're right, I didn't get to do that. The thought of mounting her in that chair did cross my mind, but Sadie was really enjoying what I was doing for her. So, I didn't change it up."

"If I hadn't left, though..."

"Don't blame yourself for that," I reply. "Look, there could be other opportunities if we stick around here, but we need to get ourselves conditioned for living like this. We can't half-assed do this if we are going to stay in this community. We have to make a choice. Do we give in or get out?" My question might seem a little too direct for Marcy after what she has shared with me, but we need to come to an agreement as to what will happen from now on. If she doesn't want to continue to have sex with others, we need to leave. Otherwise, the gated community will seem a little too weird to us.

Marcy looks out the window again as she asks, "What should we do next if we stay? How do we get me into this thing a little better?"

"Well, I have an idea, but it would require you to lose a little of your modesty, my love. You will need to be ready to show off for people." Pausing for her to think on that a moment, I add, "You didn't take your clothes off over at the Campbell's house. That was the first sign that you were a little too worried about what was happening. If you want to stay and try to make things work out here, you will need to be willing to show off what you have, Marcy."

"I did that the other night, Jake."

"I know, and it surprised me to find out that you had done it. Still, this is an opportunity for the two of us to really experience sex in a different way, Marcy. If we're going to do this, we need to do it. What do you say? Can you do it?"

My wife turns to look at me. A slight smile begins to form on her face. "Let's try it, Jake. Let's see if we can really become a part of this place."

"That's the spirit." I give her a hug as I think about what this means for the two of us. Our sex life has been a little dry over the last few months, and now that we are here and getting to be a part of what is going on in this little gated community, I want to experience so much more. Though I think Sadie might have to stay out of my bed for now, there are others in the neighborhood who will do nicely for me. Marcy and I need to do this to make things a little spicier for our own marriage. I think this could be a real turning point in our marriage.

Chapter Eight: A Friendly Fuck

"You can do it," I tell Marcy as we stand out on our front porch. "Just let it all go." The breeze across my ball sack feels nice as I stand naked in front of our house. No one has yet noticed and I'm not sure how far we're going to get if I can't get my wife to take her bathrobe off.

"I don't know," she replies as her face turns bright red. "I've never just walked around in my birthday suit while in public."

I smile at her. "Look, they all do that sort of thing here. No one is going to call the police or security to arrest us. Let's just take a nice walk and see what happens."

"Jake, this is not the best idea you've ever had."

"Just do it, baby. Come on. What do we have to lose?" We lock eyes for a moment as she considers my words. Marcy knows that I'm right. There is very little to lose by walking around naked in a place that encourages trading spouses at their parties. "Maybe we'll see some other nudists around as well."

She laughs. "I think we likely will." Marcy unties her bathrobe and allows it to drop to the porch. Her small, perky breasts react to the breeze and her nipples tighten. I begin to get a little hard as I look over my wife's petite form.

"Here we go." I step off the porch with Marcy and we begin to walk through the neighborhood. It doesn't take long for someone to notice us.

"Hello, neighbors," Luke says from his front yard. He smiles as he watches us go by. "A nice day for a tan, isn't it?"

"A very nice day," I reply. Marcy barely looks at him as she smiles bashfully. Her waxed pussy glistens as we continue to make our way down the sidewalk. The temptation to simply fuck my wife right here, right now is so strong, but I do my best to avoid doing so.

"That's the Marcus house," Marcy tells me. "I met Natalie Marcus the other day. She's nice." We walk around the side of the house to the back yard, where both Natalie and her husband are naked and working in a small garden.

"Marcy!" The woman runs up to the edge of the yard and smiles at us. "It's good to see you." Her eyes then turn to my cock for a quick moment before she puts her attention fully on my wife. "You need to meet my husband!" We walk into their backyard to where the other man is using a small shovel to dig holes for some flower bulbs. "Paul, this is Marcy and her husband Jake." She looks at me. "It is *Jake,* right?"

I nod my head. "Yeah, I'm Jake." I reach out and shake Paul's hand. "Nice to meet you."

"Nice to meet you as well," he replies. Natalie leads my wife to the other end of the small backyard garden where they begin to work on something else. "Sorry I didn't get to meet you at the party the other night, but we were out of town."

"No problem," I reply as I try to avoid looking at his large manhood. "We're new here, so we're still getting to know everyone."

Paul chuckles. "Well, walking around like that will certainly get you acquainted with everyone here." We both laugh as Paul turns to lead me to where the women are bent over working on something. "Nice," he says as he looks at the two women's asses facing us. "Wouldn't you agree?"

"Um, yeah." I feel myself getting hard as I look at his wife's full bush. "So, flowers? All of this?"

He nods. "Natalie loves flowers, so I try to keep her happy by planting however many I can for her. She rarely comes out here to help, but she loves looking at the flowers once they bloom." Paul points to the two women. "Your wife has a full set of lips. They are very nice." I blush as I see my wife's pussy lips shining back at us.

"She's tight, too," I reply as I get harder.

"You like Natalie, don't you?" he asks as he sees my woody. "Do you want to go up and get a whiff of her?"

"Um, you mean *smell* her?" My face turns red as I look at the other man.

"Sure. She won't mind." Paul nudges me and I walk up to his wife. Her asshole is beautiful and tight as I look down at it. "Sweetheart, stay still. He wants to sniff you out, if that's okay?"

Natalie giggles. "Go for it." Hard and already pre-coming, I bend down and inhale her essence. The aroma of her pussy is sweet and alluring. I want to taste it, but it would require that I fight the forest around it to get to it.

"And you're wet." I turn to see Paul's finger inside my wife's pussy. Her face is red as she allows him to thrust his digit in and out of her. After a few plunges into her muff, he pulls his finger out and sniffs it before tasting her juices. "You're so wet already. Are you always this wet?"

"She's horny," his wife tells him.

"Me too." Paul gets close to my wife, his cock erect, and begins to run it between her soft pussy lips. "You're so smooth." His face turns a little red as he enjoys the feeling of Marcy's pussy lips over the head of his cock. "I want to fuck you, Marcy. Can I fuck you?"

My wife looks at me as I finger Natalie's pussy. She's wet as well, moaning as I move my finger in and out of her. "Fuck me too," Natalie says. I push my hardness against her wet beaver and begin to sink into her bush. At this point, Paul is pushing into Marcy as far as he can. Here we are, two couples swapping with each other in broad daylight. It doesn't take long for some of the neighbors to see what is going on. Several of them come over and watch as Paul and I enjoy the pussies of each other's wives.

"Shit," I hear Marcy say as she puts her hands on the ground to steady herself. It's obvious that she's enjoying Paul's large phallus as he fucks her. "You're deep."

"I can get deeper," he grunts as his balls ram her full labia. My wife whimpers as he finds her cervix.

"Come inside me, alright?" Natalie looks back at me, her black hair hanging over one shoulder. I grip her hips tightly and thrust hard into her, her cervix hard and inviting.

"Holy fuck," I moan as I watch her thick bush snuggle my cock and balls. I've never fucked a woman with a full set of pubes before. This is a new experience for me, and I'm glad to be having it right now.

"Oh, hell," my wife moans as she plays with her own nipples. Whatever Paul's cock is doing inside her, she's liking it. I turn to see about eight or so people watching us fuck in the backyard and it turns me on even more. My balls slap hard against Natalie as I move faster and faster inside her. Thrusting into her fuzzy muff is exciting.

"Oh...uhhhh..." Paul's face is turning red as he enjoys my wife. The idea that I have just met him and that he is fucking my wife makes my balls ache as he continues to pound Marcy's pussy. "Motherfucker. Wow...yes..." Sweat begins to bead on his forehead as Paul thrusts faster and faster. My dear wife is playing with her nipples, tugging at each one and twisting them while he humps her hard.

"Jake," Natalie moans. I can feel her tight, wet hole become even tighter as she grips my cock. "Fuck me hard, big guy. Fuck me so hard." Her legs shake as I pull hard on her hips, the head of my manhood ramming her cervix hard.

"Shit, you're tight," I tell her as I feel my jizz beginning to move from my balls to my shaft. "I love fucking other women," I groan, causing Marcy to look over at me. I get the feeling that she wants to comment on what I have just said, but she doesn't. Instead, she simply continues to enjoy the feeling of Paul's monster meat inside her tiny hole.

"Holy...ohhhhh..." Marcy suddenly comes as her lover porks her in the pussy hard. *"Nahhhh! OHHHHH!!!"* Her face turns dark red as she pulls at her nipples and looks back at Paul. This is the first time I've actually seen her come with another man, her small, firm ass turning red as he slaps it hard. *"UHHHH!!!"*

"FUCK!!!" Paul's body shakes hard as he begins to launch his manly gravy into Marcy's wet snapper. *"Ohhh...uhhh...uhhh..."* His hands grip my wife's small hips tightly as he pulls her to him while thrusting. *"SHIT!!! OHHHH!!!"* Several of the men standing nearby begin to play

with themselves as they watch him fill my wife's small hole with all of
his seed. There is so much of his spunk that some of it spills out from
between his large cock and Marcy's labia onto the ground.

"*Ohhhh...*" My body jerks hard as I spurt into Natalie's wet womb. I
can feel her begin to come at the same time, her vagina undulating as it
accepts my milky ejaculate. "*Ahhhh!!! FUCK!!!*"

"*JAKE!!! JAKE!!!*" Paul's wife squeals loudly as I push hard against
her cervix. "*FUCK!!! OHHHHH!!!*"

"Holy shit, I think he's trying to ram it through her," one of the
men in the group nearby exclaims. The others laugh as they play with
themselves. One of the women even bends over and lets a man begin to
fuck her as well. I'm not certain they are married to each other, but in
this private community I don't think that really matters.

"Oh..." I pull out of Natalie and back away as I admire the stream of
jism slowly trailing out of her furry beaver. Smiling to myself, I realize
that she will have to spend a little bit more time than most of the women
here cleaning herself up. The thick black mat around her pussy lips is
worth it, though.

Marcy stands up as some of Paul's genetic brew streams down one
of her legs. "I can't believe we just did that." She looks around and acts
as if she's a little embarrassed of what the others have seen. Of course,
everyone here is nude, so it really doesn't matter. Not one of us will pass
judgement on any other in our community since we have been taking
part in the same things as well.

"Thank you," Paul says to my wife as he takes her hand and kisses it
gently. A string of come stretches from the tip of his dick to one of the
flowers between his feet.

Marcy blushes and nods her head at him before turning to whisper
to me, "Can we go home now?" I nod and soon we are heading back to
our house.

As we walk inside, I ask her, "So, what do you think? Was it okay? I
was a little surprised by it all, myself."

My wife smiles. "I think I like this, Jake. All of this. I know that before I was a little apprehensive, but it seems like there are really good people here and they just want to experience sex together. I want to have sex as well, and who better to do that with?"

"So, you don't want to move out of here?"

Marcy giggles. "Not anymore." She walks up to me and pulls me close to her. We kiss deeply as we run our hands over each other's bodies. Surprising to me is how badly Marcy wants to be with me now even after she has orgasmed with Paul. My cock begins to get hard once again.

Chapter Nine: A Golden Opportunity

It's been three months since the last party. Marcy and I have been excitedly talking about what Sadie and Luke have told us is a *recognition ceremony* for the new couple in the community. We are the newest, so I would have to assume that they are talking about us. There's no way to know for certain what will happen tonight, but we're ready for whatever could take place at the party. Even if it involves a basket with dozens of keys.

"Are you nervous?" Marcy asks me as we walk up to the front door of our neighbors house down the street. The Campbell's are not hosting tonight's party as they did three months ago. It's the turn of a middle-aged couple known as the Rubin's.

"Not too nervous," I reply. "A little, but only because we don't know exactly what they will want to do. Of course, we didn't really know what would happen last time either."

"It was a bit of a shock," my wife agrees. "Sadie still has her eye on you."

I blush a little. "Well, we haven't done anything that you don't know about, I promise," I reply. "Like we promised each other a while back, we won't have sex with others unless we both agree to it."

"I think that's for the best," Marcy replies. She's right. This community could very easily wear out a marriage if that marriage lacked playful boundaries. We know what we can do and when we can do it now. That's put both of us more at ease since coming here more than three months ago.

We open the front door to the Rubin's house and go inside. The party is in full swing already with loud music and people gathered in large groups. There appears to be even more people at this party than there were at the last one. I recall Sadie telling us that there were some people who had to be gone for work the last time. Apparently they've made their way back home now.

"Come in, my friends," Charlie Rubin says with a smile on his face. Marcy and I haven't had sex with him or his wife Dana, but it's been obvious for some time that they would like to enjoy us in bed. I'm not opposed at all to having Dana's legs over my shoulders, but Charlie is a little boastful about his sexual abilities. This hasn't set well with Marcy. She considers him a little too full of himself.

"Thank you," I say with a nod as we make our way inside to greet the Rubin's as well as the Campbell's nearby.

"It's about time," Sadie laughs as she looks at the two of us. "You're a little late. What were you doing? Having sex in the hot tub?" I feel my face turn red as Marcy shakes her head and laughs with her new friend.

"Nah, not us. I just couldn't get Jake to finish what he was doing on the computer."

"Hey, I had work to do, alright? There's a deadline to what I do, Marcy."

"A committed man. I like that," Sadie answers.

Luke walks up and shakes my hand. "Good to see you again, buddy. It's been a couple of weeks."

"I know. There's just been so much for us to do lately. We should be good for tonight and a few more days, though. We're ready to party." My cock grows a little hard as I think about the key basket and which woman might come to my house tonight. I can't wait to see who will draw the lucky key.

"That's good, because we have something of a surprise for you." Luke winks at the two of us before he leads his wife away.

"They have been really looking forward to this," Dana says as she puts a hand on my shoulder. My manhood aches for the older, beautiful woman. I hope that I get to have sex with her tonight.

"Luke has been talking so much about it that I'm surprised the surprise hasn't gotten out," Charlie adds.

"You know what it is?" Marcy asks.

"No, not really. All they have told us is that this surprise is a new surprise. Apparently it has to do with the fact that the two of you got right into things in our gated community faster than anyone before you."

Marcy blushes. "I didn't think we moved that fast."

"Oh, you did," Dana says with a giggle. "That time you went out nude and had fun in the middle of the day with Paul and Natalie seems to have gotten their attention. Honestly, we weren't that bold when we first got here. It took us about six months to warm up to this lifestyle."

"Wow." I smile a little as I look at my wife. "All because you're the wild woman." She reaches out and slaps me across the shoulder before laughing. I'm glad to see Marcy so happy about what we have here.

"Excuse me. Let me have your attention." Luke holds up a microphone from a karaoke set at the front of the large living room.

"We told him it would work better than the little bell. It sounds better, right?" Dana asks.

"Definitely," I reply.

"As most of you already know, we have a very special new-*ish* couple with us tonight." Luke points toward us and Marcy wraps her arm around mine. She shakes a little, as do I, at the thought of what we might be asked to do.

Sadie takes the microphone from her husband. "Marcy and Jake, you have both been so much fun around here in the last three months. We have all watched you accept with open arms the lifestyle we have here. So, to show you how much we appreciate you, we have something for you." She nods at a young woman nearby who walks over to us. "This basket contains only one key, but it's a special key." Sadie pauses as we look into the basket.

"Go ahead, it's yours," the young woman says to us. I watch as Marcy reaches in and retrieves the key. She looks at it and says, "That's weird."

"It's the Golden Key," Sadie says over the microphone as she smiles at us. "This key allows you tonight to select whichever couple you want to be with." She looks across the room. "This is a new thing that we thought we would start, and if it works out, maybe we'll continue it in the future. But for now, Marcy, you and your husband will be the first to select any other couple here to swap with."

Luke takes back the microphone. "There's just one little catch."

"There always is," I say from across the large formal living room. The people around us laugh.

"The Rubin's have been so kind as to allow us the use of their guest house just out back for this. A wonderful bed has been set up and there is plenty of room for people to watch."

"Watch?" Marcy laughs nervously.

"Yes, watch. If that's alright with the two of you." Luke smiles and I get the feeling from the look on Sadie's face that this part is primarily his idea.

"Well?" I ask my wife. "Want to go for it?"

She swallows hard. "Why not? Let's do it." I look up and nod my head and there is cheering in the living room.

"So, who will it be?" Luke asks.

I turn to Marcy. "This is for you," I tell her. "You decide who you want us to take to the guest house." Looking over at the Rubin's, I ask quietly, "Would you like to have them come with us?"

"No," she says with a strained look. Poor Charlie is just not her type. Marcy begins to walk through the living room as she looks at the others gathered for this party. It takes her a minute or so, but she settles on a young couple named Heidi and Damien Bilks. The people in the living room clap and cheer us all on, Heidi's already-red cheeks becoming redder.

"And there you have it. Let's allow the two couples to go to the guest house and get comfortable before we join them." Luke motions toward the back of the house. The four of us walk to a large sliding glass door and walk out into the back yard toward the other house.

"I can't believe you chose us," Damien says as we make our way to the door of the smaller house.

Marcy turns around and looks at him. "I've had my eye on you for a while." Goosebumps rise along my neck and back and she turns and waits for him to open the door. He uses the golden key and unlocks it so that we can walk inside. As we do, we're amazed at the large room decorated with a large bed and plenty of lighting.

"Damn," I say as I shake my head. "This is really tricked out."

"Yeah, it is." Heidi's voice is quiet and reserved as she agrees with me. Her blue eyes, framed by her shoulder-length strawberry hair, mesmerize me. I can't believe that I've not really noticed her before, but she's a beautiful young woman.

"We're new too," Damien says, "But we've been here a while longer than you. I guess it's been a little harder for us to really get into things."

Marcy smiles at him. "Have you both had the chance to do much with the others yet?"

"No," Damien says nervously as he looks at his wife. "Heidi isn't sure that she likes this yet."

"Wow," I reply. "Would you rather not do this, then?"

Heidi shakes her head. "It's like ripping a bandaid off, right? That should do it, shouldn't it?" She looks from me to her husband and then at Marcy. There's concern in her expression, but at the same time she appears to be ready to do this. I get hard as I consider the fact that Damien and his wife appear to be no older than twenty-five or so.

"I think that would be best." My wife walks up to the young man and pulls his head to her. She begins to kiss him hard as her hand goes to the bulge inside his pants. Heidi's eyes grow wide.

"Holy shit, honey," I say under my breath as I watch her pull down Damien's pants and shove his cock into her mouth. Damien doesn't have time to stop her as she begins to gobble down all nine inches or more of his large phallus.

Heidi looks at me nervously. "I can't do that so well."

I smile. "Then I'll be gentle, okay? I'll stop at any point if you tell me to." Heidi nods her head as I approach her. She has her small hands balled into fists as she is nervous about our encounter. I need to treat her like it's her first time, though I know it's not. For me, this could be difficult.

"Oh, Marcy," the other man moans as he puts his hands on my wife's head. At this point, the door of the guest house opens and some of the people from the party make their way inside. There appear to be some others standing outside in the yard while drinking and talking. Perhaps they've seen this enough that they don't necessarily need to come in here and watch.

I lead Heidi to the bed and gently sit her down. Bending down, I kiss her lips softly, the flavor of cherry lip gloss filling my mouth as I do. "I'll go slowly," I promise again. Moving to her neck, I begin to nibble at it, causing goosebumps to break out there. Though she is bashful about our encounter, Heidi's hands move up to my head and her fingers begin to make their way through my hair. I love the way she smells and the way her skin feels as I continue to kiss her.

Marcy stands to her feet and begins to undress. Her lover does the same, the two of them very quickly naked and against each other as they get on one side of the bed. I continue to kiss and fondle Heidi nearby as I work her up to where she will be more comfortable with doing more.

"Jake," Heidi whispers into my ear. "Don't come inside me, okay? Anywhere but inside me."

My cock deflates just a little as I pull back and look into her intensely blue eyes. Heidi is the sort of woman a man could easily fall in love with. She's beautiful and very sweet. I can see why Damien married her. I can also see why Marcy affects him so much. I simply nod my head as I smile at Heidi.

"Damien," Marcy moans as the young man eats her pussy beside us. Heidi looks over at them and I can tell that she's bothered by her husband enjoying another woman's twat.

I reach over and gently guide her head toward me. "It's just the two of us, okay?" I reach down and pull on the bottom of her tee shirt. Heidi allows me to lift it over her head, though she seems shy as she crosses her bra-covered chest. "Just us," I say again as I reach between her breasts and unfasten her bra. She allows me to pull it away to reveal two C-cup breasts with small, light-pink nipples that harden once the air of the room meets them. My manhood throbs as I look at them and the small freckles between her breasts.

"Be easy with me," she pleads.

"I will." I bend down and kiss her full breasts for a moment before turning my attention to her nipples. Drawing one into my mouth, I gently lick and suck on it, causing her small body to quiver. Heidi makes an almost imperceptible whimper as she puts her hands on my head and intertwines her fingers into my hair. She likes what I am doing to her as we sit beside her husband and my wife.

The bed begins to shake as Damien shoves his long, fleshy sword into my wife's sheath. "Uh...holy shit..." Marcy grips the covers tightly as he rams his cock in and out of her. Her eyes close as she bites her lower lip and just enjoys the feeling of him inside her. Damien is a man who has had mostly vanilla sex since marrying Heidi, and now he's determined to release whatever pent-up sexual angst he has.

"You're tight," he growls as he fucks my wife. "Holy fuck, you're so damned tight." He begins to sweat across his muscular chest as he enjoys my wife's vagina around his manhood.

"It's just us," I say as I turn Heidi's face toward me again. I help her to her feet and she begins to lift my shirt as well. We help each other with our pants and soon we stand before each other completely nude.

She reaches slowly for my cock and takes hold of it with one hand. I feel my body flex a little as she carefully squeezes it. "I can't suck it very well," she tells me. "I gag a little and I can't swallow." Her embarrassment causes me to feel for her.

"Just kiss it," I tell her. Heidi nods her head as I sit down on the bed. She bends over and presses her lips against the head of my cock. I pre-come a little and it coats her lips. Heidi then opens her mouth and takes me part way inside. My body shakes as her tongue rolls across the tip of my dick.

"Is this good?" she says when she looks up at me a moment later.

"Yeah, it's good," I tell her. "You don't do this much, do you?" A look of disappointment fills her face.

"I'm sorry." She crosses her arms and looks around the room at the other people.

"It's okay." I lay her in the bed beside my wife. Opening her legs, I go down and inhale her sweet essence. Heidi's waxed beaver is lovely, her lips a light pink and ready for me. As I begin to taste her, the young woman's body bucks.

"Too much," she tells me. "Please."

Damien looks at me and says, "She doesn't like to come that way."

I get up and look at him. "You know, I'll bet Marcy would love you to put her against the wall." His eyes light up and he looks down at my wife. She would have noticed had she not been playing with her own nipples, her eyes closed. I watch as Damien lifts my wife from the bed as she remains on his cock. He carries her to a wall and puts her against it as he continues to push in and out of her. The new angle seems to get the both of them really going again.

I go back down on Heidi. My tongue twirls around her small clit before moving between her labia and into her pussy. She bucks again and begins to push on my head, but I ignore her. Instead, I slide two fingers into her and look for her G-spot as I keep lapping at her wetness.

"*Ooooohh...*" I think I've found it. Heidi stops pushing at my head and instead begins to breathe hard and fast. "*Uhhhh...UHHHH!!!*" The orgasm is sudden and unexpected on my part as the young woman comes hard. Her sweet nectar gushes from her pussy as she ejaculates all over my face and head.

"A gusher!" someone says in the room. I can hear others fucking each other around the small house, the sounds of flesh on flesh filling the air. My cock hard, I move around and press it against her wet opening before entering Heidi's pussy.

"Jake," she says while catching her breath. "What was that?"

"One hell of an orgasm," I tell her as I put her legs back and look for her G-spot with my cock. Swollen and knobby, I find it easily and begin to stroke back and forth across it.

"Fuck, *again?* I can't..." Her face turns red as her body tenses. "*UHHHH!!! FUCK!!!*" Heidi comes for a second time to my surprise as I move in and out of her hard, striking her low cervix as I do. "*Ahhhh...UHHHH!!!*" This time, her orgasm is more intense as she squirts again. Her sticky love nectar coats my cock and abdomen as I lift her ass from the bed. Something tells me that Damien has never had this experience with her. Instead of a bashful prude, he has a wildcat just waiting for an excuse to come out and play.

"*OHHHH...*" He comes inside my wife as he presses her hard against the wall, her knees over his shoulders. "*Ahhh...ahhhh...ohhhh...*"

"*Damien!*" Marcy squeals as their bodies wriggle around together against the wall. Though I would normally turn and watch my wife with the other man, I'm more interested in Heidi and what might happen next.

"I'm getting close. I'll pull out when I get there," I tell the young wife.

She pants heavily as her body shudders. "I'm going to come again too," she tells me. Her pussy tightens around my cock as she screams out, "*COME INSIDE ME!!! COME INSIDE ME, JAKE!!!*"

I thrust hard as I feel myself begin to spurt. Instead of pulling out, I coat her cervix with my seed. "*Uhhhh...ohhhhh...OHHHH!!!*" My orgasm is intense as Heidi again squirts all over me. "*UHHH!!!*

FUCK!!!" Her pussy has a tight grip on me as I thrust hard in and out of her. I don't think I've ever come so hard with anyone else before.

"AHHHH...FUCK!!! FUCK!!! MOTHERFUCKER!!!" Heidi sounds almost possessed as she comes with me for the third time tonight. Her body is red now and I wonder if she will pass out from the intense orgasm. Her husband is watching nearby after pulling out of my wife. It's obvious that he hasn't seen Heidi like this before.

After we finish, I pull out of the young wife and roll over on the bed to my back. My spent jism is slowly making its way out of her tight, full labia as she smiles at me.

"Never before..." It's all she says as she looks over at Damien. They smile at each other and I can see that this will end up leading to more fun for them now that he has seen her give in so willingly to someone else. It's my hope that they will have a great sex life from this point on. I know Marcy and I do.

"Fun, huh?" Sadie says as she walks up to the bed. "That was like nothing I've seen before."

"The Golden Key is here to stay," Luke laughs from nearby. I turn and look at Marcy and smile at her. She's happy and content after Damien has filled her full of his man gravy. This has been the most eventful party we have ever been to. Bar none.

Chapter Ten: A Great Decision

"I would have never guessed that you would have gotten Heidi to do anything at all," Marcy giggles as we walk in the park just outside of our gated community.

I laugh. "You picked them not just because of Damien, but you thought that I wouldn't be getting much from her."

She gives me a wry look. "I suppose I'm still dealing with my own insecurities in all this, Jake," my wife admits. "I knew Damien was what I wanted, but Heidi..." Marcy laughs. "Who would have thought that you would have unlocked something in her like you did?"

"I'm sure Damien is reaping the rewards."

"He told me that he is," she replies, "But he still hasn't gotten her to come three times in one night the way you did. What did you do to her, Jake?" Marcy seems very interested in my response.

"Well, I just took things slower with her. There wasn't going to be any of the fast and hard stuff with us. As a matter of fact, I get the feeling that Damien likes to go to that playbook the most. It's probably why he doesn't get the same results from his own wife."

Marcy blushes. "I like that style, though."

"Oh, I know you do." We both laugh.

My wife thinks for a moment and tells me, "I'm trying to get Jancy and Ted Faulkner to move here in a couple of months."

"Jancy and Ted?" I raise an eyebrow. "They live in Canada, honey. They're nowhere near Florida."

"I know, but they are both going to be working from home for the foreseeable future. They might as well come down here to live near us. There are three houses for sale right now." She smiles as she winks at me.

Shaking my head, I reply, "You've had your eyes on Ted for a long time, haven't you? Even before we moved here."

"He's nice," Marcy says in a shy way.

"Wow, baby. I'm really surprised." I laugh as I look at my beautiful wife. She surprises me now that we have gotten comfortable with our new life together.

"Surprised that we made such a great decision?" she asks as she gets close to me and puts her arms around me.

"Well, okay, sure. But, *Ted?*"

"He grows on a girl," she tells me as we begin to walk again. "Just like you grew on me."

"What? It was love at first sight when we met, my love."

"Sure it was, sweetheart. Sure it was." We continue our walk as we consider ourselves fortunate to have found such a wonderful gated community. In just three months we'll have another community party, and it wouldn't surprise me if Marcy actually convinces our friends to move here. That means it's possible, if not highly likely, that we'll fuck our friends eventually. Though that's the sort of thinking that I would have dismissed at one time, I'm now convinced of our desires to have sex for the fun of sex. There's nothing wrong with that, after all.

THE END

Don't miss out!

Visit the website below and you can sign up to receive emails whenever Karly Violet publishes a new book. There's no charge and no obligation.

https://books2read.com/r/B-A-GIXE-YCTQB

BOOKS 2 READ

Connecting independent readers to independent writers.

Did you love *Wife Swapping Party - A Wife Watching Multiple Partner Hotwife Romance Novel*? Then you should read *Hotwife Affair In Lockdown - A Hotwife Multiple Partner Wife Watching Romance Novel*[1] by Karly Violet!

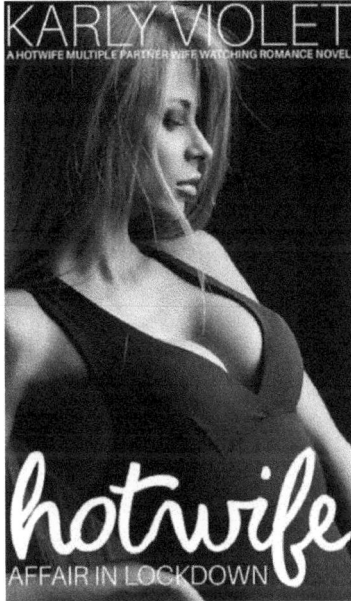

Beautiful Wife Finds A Way To Comfort Her Loneliness During The Pandemic While Her Husband Is Stranded Overseas

The early stages of the pandemic **separated many married couples.**

And this was no different for Leyland and his wife Karie.

The successful husband was travelling on business from the States to London.

But as he neared the end of his trip and the pandemic was gripping the world, non-essential flights were grounded and Leyland found himself stranded thousands of miles away from his beautiful wife.

---

1. https://books2read.com/u/3JRB6A

2. https://books2read.com/u/3JRB6A

The uncertainty of when Leyland would return back home didn't concern him, he knew their marriage would strengthen further.

Karie believed this too...........**until she started to get lonely.**

And the longer Leyland was away, the more the **stunning housewife yearned for intimacy.**

So much so that neighbours started to notice as men started to visit Karie almost daily.

Can a lonely housewife's cheating ways ever be forgiven?

This 20,000 word scorching hot novel features a lonely wife exploring way to comfort her loneliness whilst her husband is stranded overseas in the midst of the pandemic!

Read more at https://www.patreon.com/karlyviolet.

About the Author

Sign up to my mailing list to receive the two free epilogues for 'A Hotwife Adventure' and 'Hotwife Training' and to stay up to date on all of my latest releases! http://eepurl.com/c3ICWf Sign up to my Patreon account and receive exclusive Hotwife stories every month and sexy scenes every week! https://www.patreon.com/karlyviolet

Read more at https://www.patreon.com/karlyviolet.

About the Publisher

Milton Keynes UK
Ingram Content Group UK Ltd.
UKHW040833120224
437701UK00001B/101